D1135347

About the Author

Graham Clarke is a writer, he likes football, walking and rugby. He comes from Newcastle and lives in Northumberland. He supports Liverpool football club and Newcastle Falcons rugby union football club. His favourite food is chilli and rice. His favourite drink is milk.

Graham Clarke

FLUFFY RABBIT AND FRIENDS

AUSTIN MACAULEY
PUBLISHERS LTD.

A CIP catalogue record for this title is available from the British Library.

ISBN 9781785543395 (Paperback)
ISBN 9781785543401 (Hardback)
ISBN 9781785543418 (E-Book)

www.austinmacauley.com

First Published (2016)
Austin Macauley Publishers Ltd.
25 Canada Square
Canary Wharf
London
E14 5LQ

In a very green land, there lives a rabbit who is very fluffy. His name, therefore, is Fluffy Rabbit and we meet him as he is on his way to meet up with his friends, all of whom he loves.

"All of my friends are intriguing characters," he tells us. "Take Foley McFluffy, the cat, for instance. He's into doing weird and funny things. Then there's Trips Spirt; like Foley, she is also a cat and she likes to run around like a crazy cat. Well, that's what she is. Then there's Barney, the dog. He's ridiculously strong. Such is his strength, he once pulled a human to the ground. There's also Chalky, the hamster, who loves to be playful in his hamster ball. Another of my friends is Pip, the horse, who likes to eat Polo mints and roam around in fields."

So these are Fluffy's friends and now we are going to share in some of their latest adventures.

Fluffy Rabbit had just arrived to hang out with his unique bunch of friends.

"Hey, Foley, my feline dude," Fluffy said, with a wink at Foley.

"Hey, Fluffy, fluffy twerp," joked Foley.

"You cheeky sod!" Fluffy replied and then grinned at Trips, revealing his long, sharp front teeth. "Hey, Trips, my feline dude."

Trips smiled. "Hi, Fluffy."

"Hey, Barney, give me an arm wrestle," Fluffy challenged the dog.

Barney showed his long, pink tongue. "No prob, Fluffy. C'mon, Big Ears."

Fluffy was proud of his tall, fluffy ears and was not offended by Barney's reference to them. He had never been successful in beating Barney at arm wrestling but he was always ready to take him on. Of course, he lost yet again, and in two seconds flat.

"Damn, you win again," he cursed. "Maybe I'll win next time."

"With my strength, Fluffy? In your dreams, I think," Barney said, looking very pleased with himself.

Fluffy laughed and waved a paw at Chalky. "Hey, Chalky, my ball-loving rodent."

"Hi, Fluffy," Chalky replied, blowing out his fat little cheeks.

"Hey, Pip! You going to be horsin' around?"

Pip responded with a toss of his head, rolling his big brown eyes. "Neigh," he said, smiling and revealing his large, hay-munching teeth.

"So, what shall we do?" Fluffy asked his friends.

"I think we should go to Animal Woods," suggested Foley.

"Good idea, my feline dude," Fluffy replied. "All agreed?"

"Yeah," his friends replied. "Agreed."

Fluffy, Foley, Barney, Chalky, Pip and Trips set off on their journey to Animal Woods, one of their favourite haunts.

"Wow, this is a good journey so far," Fluffy said to his friends.

All his friends murmured their agreement.

"So, tell us a joke, Foley," Fluffy said.

"Okay." Foley thought for a moment. "What's long and fluffy and looks like a fox's tail?"

Fluffy, Trips, Pip, Barney and Chalky looked at each other. None of them had an answer.

"We're not sure," they replied.

"Give up?"

"Give up."

"My tail, of course," Foley said.

His friends all laughed together.

"You're a funny dude," Barney said.

Foley looked smug. "Yeah, I know."

"We're going on a trip, we're going on a trip, my name is Trips and we're going on a trip," sang Trips.

The others smiled at Trips and then they progressed a bit further on their journey to Animal Woods.

They approached a river with stepping stones.

"Hey, let's cross these stepping stones," Fluffy suggested to his friends. "I'll go last and lie down across the stones, so that Chalky can roll over me."

"Right," thought Foley, "time to do a roly-poly when I cross these stepping stones." He ran across the stones and then finished with a forward roll.

Barney ran across the stepping stones and Pip galloped after him. Fluffy then lay down on the first couple of stepping stones and Chalky, in his hamster ball, rolled over him. They repeated the procedure until they had covered all the stepping stones and joined their friends on the other side of the river.

Continuing their journey, they passed some sheep in an open field.

"Lamb chops," Foley called out as they walked by.

Barney grinned. "That was a good one, Foley."

"So, Chalky, how was it, rolling over me?" Fluffy asked.

"It was awesome," Chalky replied, his eyes wide with excitement.

Fluffy turned to the others. "How are you all enjoying your journey so far?" he asked.

"It's fabulous," they all agreed.

As they continued their journey, they passed more green fields.

"Ah, the rich green of the countryside is so good to see," Barney remarked.

The friends all murmured their approval. As they walked, a farm came into view and they saw two bantams scratching about as they approached.

"It's rock and roll time," said Foley, and he ran over to the nearest bantam and bit its head off. He gobbled up the head immediately and then ate the rest of the bird.

Trips made a dash for the other bantam and quickly bit off its head, and then ate the remains in the same way.

"That was one tasty birdie," Trips said, licking his lips.

Fluffy and the others all chuckled at that, and before they continued their journey, Fluffy, Chalky, Pip and Barney ate some refreshing grass, with Chalky taking mouthfuls through the holes in his ball.

As they set off again, some birds flew overhead.

Foley looked up at them. "Those birds are so lucky I'm on the ground," he said, "or they would be in my stomach."

The friends walked steadily for half an hour, covering a lot of land. Then they came upon a wounded red squirrel.

"Oh, my God," Fluffy exclaimed. "He looks to be in a bad way. We should help him, guys."

"Yeah," they all agreed. "We will do what we can to help."

Fluffy picked some strong blades of grass. "Right. I am going to stitch this red squirrel's wound. Trips, I will need to use your claws as a needle when I say so, okay?"

"Oh yes, of course," Trips agreed.

"Claw in wound NOW," ordered Fluffy.

Trip activated her sharp claws and used them to pierce holes around the squirrel's wound. As soon as she withdrew her claws, Fluffy threaded the blades of grass through the holes and tied them securely, sealing the wound.

The red squirrel winced as Fluffy tied the blades of grass but he was grateful.

"Thanks for that," he said. "My name's Nutty, by the way."

"You're welcome," said Fluffy and Trips. "Nice to meet you, Nutty."

"Yeah, nice to meet you," the others agreed, and they all told him their names.

"So … can I join your team?" Nutty asked.

"Yeah, why not?"

"Oh, it is good to know I've got friends."

"Who attacked you?" Fluffy asked him.

"A gang of grey squirrels. They took the lives of my family as well," Nutty replied sadly.

"That's terrible," Fluffy said. "Right, we'll organise a war against them."

"I'd appreciate that," Nutty said. "And I'd like to fight as well."

"That's good to hear," Fluffy replied. "Be careful not to pull those stitches apart, though."

They grouped together to discuss and plan their moves in the upcoming war, and when they had decided on a plan of action, they went off to hunt the grey squirrels. After half an hour, they found them. There were thousands of them.

Pip rolled his brown eyes. "Oh, my goodness," he breathed, "we are vastly outnumbered!"

Fluffy agreed. "Yes, Pip, it will be a difficult but quite unique achievement to beat them. But stranger things have happened in the world than this, you know."

"Yeah, you bet we can win," Foley declared.

Thousands of pairs of grey squirrels' eyes were watching Fluffy and his friends as they approached.

"Oh, look, they must have come to take revenge for what we did to that red squirrel and his family," said one of them, whiskers twitching uncertainly.

"Huh," said another, "so what?" He shouted to Fluffy and his friends, "What are you waiting for? Come and have a go, if you think you're strong enough!"

That spurred Fluffy on. "Right, friends; let's attack. Forward!"

Fluffy and friends advanced towards the grey squirrels, ready to attack. Pip's heavy metal shoes were a really useful weapon. A grey squirrel made an attack on Foley, not realising what powerful paws Foley had. One punch from the strong cat soon floored him. Then Nutty hit a grey squirrel, but was quickly hit back.

Trips started hissing at one of the grey squirrels; he lashed out at her, but she retaliated, leaving him in pain. Chalky, somewhat protected inside his ball, rolled towards one of the greys, bowling him over.

"Strike!" Chalky called, puffing his cheeks out in a grin.

Barney then ran towards several squirrels and knocked them all over. Then Fluffy took a run at a grey squirrel and knocked it down. "Yes!" said Fluffy, pleased with himself.

The fighting continued for a while, but the squirrels were making no progress and decided to retreat.

"Yes!" shouted Fluffy again, watching the grey squirrels scamper away. "We've won the first part of the war."

"Yeah," Foley agreed. "We have."

"So, how was it, getting back at those scumbags?" Fluffy asked Nutty.

Nutty's eyes were shining. "Awesome," he answered.

Fluffy looked at his other friends. "How was it for the rest of you?"

"Cool."

"Good."

"Way to go!"

"Right, then let's set off to find those pesky grey squirrels … yeah?"

"Yeah!"

As they all moved off to hunt down the grey squirrels, Fluffy and his friends began to chant, "We're going to win this war because losing would be such a bore."

"I'm going to beat loads of grey squirrels to a bloody mess," thought Foley.

"I'm going to go and hit the grey squirrels," thought Nutty.

Fluffy saw the grey squirrels in the distance. "There they are," he said, pointing them out to his friends.

"Right," said Foley, "let's go and catch them."

Fluffy and friends ran full pelt towards the grey squirrels, intending to catch them. The squirrels turned and ran, tails flying, trying to escape. But they were not fast enough for Fluffy and his friends, who grabbed their tails and then pounced upon them. Foley was in his element and beat one to a bloody pulp, before doing the same to several others.

"Yeah," he cried, "I love the power of violence."

Chalky was busy knocking down scores of the squirrels.

"Take that, you animal bowling pins," he shouted as they went flying.

Pip galloped towards the grey squirrels, kick-boxing them to the ground. Trips jumped on one of them, hitting it senseless, and Barney charged towards them, knocking them all out with his amazing strength. Fluffy lashed out at those within reach, sending them reeling.

"Yeah," Fluffy said, "that made me feel happy!"

"Let's fight them some more," urged Barney, flexing his huge muscles.

"Yeah," the friends chorused and advanced to the grey squirrels once again. This time the grey squirrels started throwing punches, so Fluffy and his friends retaliated with fists, hooves and paws.

"Woo-hoo, this is so much fun, getting back at these murderous scumbags," Fluffy shouted to his friends. "How is it for you?"

Fluffy's friends said they were having great fun. Chalky said he was having a ball and everyone laughed. Then they began to lift the grey squirrels up and slam them hard on the ground.

"Brings a whole new meaning to slam-dunk," grinned Fluffy.

His friends laughed and continued to throw punches at the grey squirrels.

"In your face!" shouted Nutty, punching one of them in the face.

"Feel my claws," Foley growled, scratching one of them in the face, drawing blood.

"Fine move," Fluffy said as the victim turned away, holding his face.

"Yes, it was," Foley replied with a smug grin.

Barney was still throwing some hefty punches, while Chalky was rolling back and forth, knocking the squirrels over.

"Yes … I am so good at bowling people over," he said as he toppled another one.

Pip galloped towards a group of squirrels. They froze in terror, unable to move, and he kicked them to the ground.

Trips ran after the squirrels, easily catching and attacking them. "Ha, take that!" she spat, using her sharp claws.

There followed a lot of punching by the grey squirrels, Fluffy and his friends. Loose teeth were flying about and noses were bleeding when Fluffy shouted, "Back off now!" in self-defence.

"Yeah, back off!" Fluffy's friends shouted, supportively.

Suddenly, the grey squirrels ran away, leading Fluffy and his friends on a chase.

"We're going to catch you!" Fluffy shouted.

"In your dreams, rabbit," one of them shouted cheekily and scampered up a tree. The other grey squirrels flew up after him, but Foley, Trips and Nutty followed, quickly chasing them back down. They ran straight into Pip, Chalky, Barney and Fluffy, who attacked them again.

The grey squirrels launched another attack and then ran away fast, knowing that Foley, Nutty and Trips were streaking back down the tree to make it harder to fight them.

"Come on," Fluffy yelled to his friends. "After them!" As they pursued the grey squirrels, he shouted, "We're going to catch you again and when we do, it won't be pretty!"

The grey squirrels approached a huge puddle and had no option but to splash through it. Fluffy and his friends did the same, hot on the heels of their enemies.

"We're closing in on you!" Fluffy warned.

In the next few seconds, they caught the grey squirrels and began hitting them.

"Stop!" squealed one of them.

"You deserve to have a pasting for being scumbag murderers," Fluffy replied. "Don't stop, my friends, carry on giving them a beating."

The attack continued until the grey squirrels again ran off towards a heap of logs, which they scrambled over, tails aloft.

Fluffy and his friends pursued them over the logs, Pip and Barney both clearing them with one jump.

"I love the thrill of the chase," Fluffy said, his white fluffy tail bobbing as he ran.

"Yeah, me too," Foley agreed, as they caught up with the grey squirrels yet again and began to punch them.

"Get off!" they protested. With a concerted effort, the grey squirrels somehow managed to fend off Fluffy and his friends and ran away.

But Fluffy and friends ran after them.

"We're on their tail," Foley said.

"Yeah, we're going to catch them," Fluffy replied.

"Just try and keep up with us, if you can," one shouted over his shoulder.

"We've already done so several times," said Fluffy, "so that won't be a problem."

Fluffy and friends soon gained ground on the grey squirrels and there was another tussle, but the grey squirrels squirmed free this time and took off again.

"Let's chase after them again," Fluffy said.

His friends agreed and they all gave chase again.

"Ah," Fluffy remarked, "it's good to be running with the air in my fur and enjoying a chase as well."

"Yeah," agreed his friends.

"We're gaining ground on them," Foley said, and the group tried to catch them, but this time, the grey squirrels pushed them out of the way and ran off, disappearing from view.

Fluffy and friends ran in the direction they had last seen the grey squirrels, but there was no sign of them.

"Damn! They must have hidden somewhere," Fluffy said, vexed at losing them so easily. "Spread out, they can't have gone far."

The friends formed a somewhat higgledy-piggledy line and went forward, looking all around and listening for the snap of a twig. They advanced about thirty metres, but there was no sign of the grey squirrels.

Fluffy was impatient. "Where are they?" he grumbled.

Then Foley spotted them and pointed. "There they are; over there, look."

"C'mon, what are we waiting for? After them," Fluffy replied, breaking into a run, gathering speed as he went.

They all began to run; Chalky's ball was turning at an amazing speed and Pip was at the gallop.

The grey squirrels saw them and ran, trying to hide in the forest, but Fluffy and his friends were closing in and they very soon caught them.

"I'm sick of you lot trying to escape punishment, you murderous scumbags," Fluffy shouted, throwing punches at those nearest to him.

"Yeah," said Foley, "I'm sick of you, too."

The fighting continued, with Fluffy and his friends and the grey squirrels all punching and kicking.

"We are going to win," Fluffy told the grey squirrels.

"Never. You haven't won yet," said one of them.

Fluffy and his friends jumped on the grey squirrels, thumping them, but the squirrels hit back and then managed to get free again.

"After them," cried Fluffy and he and his friends raced after the grey squirrels.

The grey squirrels gathered up some sticks as they ran, and threw them in the way of Fluffy and his friends, but they were no hindrance.

"We've overcome your obstacles," Fluffy said, "and now we're on your tail."

"We'll have more for you lot," one of the squirrels retorted, sprinting away with the rest of them.

Seeing a load of leaves on the ground, the grey squirrels then gathered them up and flung them at their pursuers.

Fluffy and his friends whacked them away and continued their chase, but the squirrels managed to stay ahead.

The grey squirrels passed a lake. A few seconds later, Fluffy and his friends ran past the lake. Some pigeons flew overhead.

"Having a fight, are you?" one of them asked.

"Mind your own business," snapped one of the grey squirrels.

"Yeah, mate, we are," Fluffy replied.

On and on went the squirrels and Fluffy and his friends continued to chase them. They ran over mole hills, tree roots, fallen branches and all sorts of hazards. Then they came to a road and the squirrels ran across it. Fluffy and friends did likewise and reached the other side just before a car sped past.

"Wow," Foley said, "it's a good job we managed to cross the road, otherwise we would have been squished!"

Fluffy and friends all laughed at what Foley had said, and after putting on a spurt, caught up with the grey squirrels again.

Another fight took place, with both sides hitting each other, and suddenly, the grey squirrels scampered away again, disappearing from sight.

"Damn, they've gone again," Fluffy groaned. "Can anyone see them?"

They all looked around, but no one could see them anywhere. The grey squirrels had gone through a mole hill and into a mole tunnel. However, the moles didn't want them invading their space and goaded them out. Once out, the squirrels kept running, but they had been spotted.

"I see them!" Foley said.

"So do we," Fluffy and the others replied.

The chase was on again and Fluffy and friends were gaining ground. They caught the grey squirrels and began to attack them. The squirrels then launched themselves into Fluffy and his friends and the fighting continued.

"Take this!" Fluffy yelled as he hit one of the grey squirrels.

"You take this!" the squirrel replied and hit Fluffy back.

Fluffy and his friends were throwing punches and the squirrels were punching back until they suddenly ran away.

"Come on," Fluffy urged his friends, "let's keep on their tail!"

The grey squirrels approached a country bridge and crossed it. Fluffy and friends also crossed it, staying on the tail of the squirrels.

"We're closing in on you," Fluffy shouted.

"You've still got to catch us," one of the squirrels replied.

"And we will."

Fluffy and his friends did catch the grey squirrels and began to give them a beating.

"Stop! Get off us!" the squirrels ordered.

"No way."

So the grey squirrels fought back and again they got away from Fluffy and his friends, running faster than ever before and soon disappeared from sight.

"Okay, we'll have to try and find them," Fluffy said.

"Yeah, but where can they be?" asked Foley.

Fluffy noticed a mail train pulling away in the distance.

Foley also noticed the train. "Do you think the grey squirrels got on that train?" he asked.

Fluffy nodded. "Yes, Foley, I think they did. Let's run to the station to catch the next train … yeah?"

Fluffy's friends agreed with a passion. "Yeah!" they chorused.

So, Fluffy and his friends ran to the station and arrived on the platform, just in time to see a train departing.

"Bother," Fluffy grumbled. "Just missed one; that's a nuisance."

However, another train pulled into the station fifteen minutes later and as it stopped, they all jumped into the nearest carriage. They rode as far as the next station and then got out. None of them had a ticket and no one asked them for one.

Looking around, the friends noticed a forest of nut trees nearby.

Fluffy pointed. "They must have gone there," he surmised. "Where else would battle-weary, hungry grey squirrels go?"

"Yeah, you're so right," the others agreed.

The friends all hurried to the forest and, as expected, the grey squirrels were up in a clump of nut trees, feasting. They surrounded the clump of trees so that the squirrels could not escape.

The grey squirrels had an unpleasant surprise when they looked down to see Fluffy and his friends waiting for them below.

"Yeah, we've found you," Fluffy called up to them, looking very pleased with himself.

"Don't expect us to come down," one of the squirrels shouted from a branch.

"Okay, but we're certain you will, though."

"We'll see about that," said another grey squirrel.

Just then, a flock of large seagulls flew overhead.

"Hey, Seagulls," one of the squirrels called, we need a lift out of here fast. Come down and carry us as far away as you can?"

The seagulls squawked and chattered between themselves and then agreed to the squirrels' request.

"Alright, hold on, we're coming."

As the seagulls flew in close to the nut trees, the grey squirrels leapt onto the birds' broad backs and were carried away.

Fluffy and friends were gobsmacked.

"Well, I was not expecting that," Fluffy said, looking after the fast flying seagulls carrying their cargo of grey squirrels.

"No," his friends agreed, following his gaze. "What do we do now, Fluffy?"

"Go after them, of course. The seagulls will have to drop them eventually."

So, Fluffy and his friends went in hot pursuit of the grey squirrels and after about half an hour they came upon them in a park, where the seagulls had landed and left their passengers.

"There they are," Fluffy said. "Right, let's go and catch them."

"Yeah!" shouted his friends, and they moved in on the grey squirrels and began beating them.

"Back off!" the grey squirrels yelled, "Get off us!"

Fluffy and his friends paused momentarily and in that short time, the grey squirrels got away again.

"Oh!" Fluffy gasped and then blew out his whiskers with frustration.

"Yeah, I'm frustrated as well," said Foley.

"Me, too," Trips said, echoed by Pip, Barney, Chalky and Nutty.

The friends set off after the grey squirrels and soon began to gain ground on them.

"We're closing in," Fluffy warned.

There was no reply from the grey squirrels, but they increased their speed and were soon out of sight again.

"Come on," Fluffy urged, "don't let them get away now!"

The friends ran as fast as they could in the direction the squirrels had gone, unaware that their enemies had stopped to gather stones and were ready to attack them.

Fluffy spotted them in the distance. "Ah, there they are; we'll have them."

"Can you see what they are doing, Fluffy?" asked Foley.

"No, Foley, they're too far away. But it looks as if they are up to something. Shall we go after them?"

"Yeah!" shouted his friends in unison, and off they went again, running towards the grey squirrels, ready to fight them.

As they approached, the grey squirrels pelted them with the stones and they had to shield themselves with their paws and hooves. Chalky thought there was a freak hailstorm clattering down on his ball. Those who could, picked up the stones and hurled them back at the grey squirrels, but none was hit as they all ran away again.

Fluffy wasted no time in leading another pursuit of the grey squirrels. "Come on," he urged his friends, "let's get after them before they give us the slip again."

"Yeah!" shouted his friends, all firmly behind him and ready to fight.

"We're closing in," Fluffy shouted as they caught up with the grey squirrels.

"Try and catch us, then," one shouted back.

"We will," Fluffy replied and within seconds he and his friends had caught the squirrels and began fighting.

The grey squirrels fought back, and were again able to run away.

"After them!" Fluffy cried.

"Yeah," his friends answered enthusiastically.

The chase began again and Fluffy and friends were closing in nicely, when the grey squirrels gathered speed and disappeared from sight.

"Oh, damn it, we've lost them again," Fluffy said despondently. "Let's have a look round; they can't be far away."

Fluffy and his friends began searching for the grey squirrels, but without any luck.

"I can't see them," said Fluffy.

"I can't see them, either," Foley added.

Nutty, Chalky, Trips, Pip and Barney all shook their heads and looked completely baffled.

Fluffy pointed ahead. "Well, let's make a move in that direction, where we last saw them."

"Yeah," his friends agreed, and they set off again to find the grey squirrels.

The grey squirrels were waiting for Fluffy and his friends with sharp sticks that they had collected. They were ready for them.

"Oh boy," said Fluffy as they approached the grey squirrels and saw their sharp weapons.

His friends regarded the squirrels with caution; what were they going to do?

They soon found out. The grey squirrels ran towards Fluffy and his friends, trying to attack them with the sharp sticks, but Fluffy and his friends managed to fend them off. Then they ran away.

"Don't come back!" yelled one of the grey squirrels as Fluffy and his friends made a hasty exit.

But Fluffy and his friends were not running away; they had gone to hunt for some sharp sticks, sharper than those wielded by the grey squirrels. They soon had a good collection of sticks to fight the squirrels with.

"Right," said Fluffy, pleased with their find, "let's take the fight back to the grey squirrels."

"Yeah!" shouted his enthusiastic friends.

Fluffy and friends ran back to the grey squirrels. When they approached, the squirrels ran towards them with their sticks raised, ready to fight.

"We're going to beat you," said the grey squirrels.

"No, we are going to beat you," Fluffy replied.

Quite a noisy battle followed as grey squirrels clashed sticks with Fluffy and his friends for about half an hour. Then a heavy storm blew up and the power of the wind forced the fighters apart. They were blown so far away, that they lost sight of each other.

"Damn!" the grey squirrels cursed with frustration.

"Damn!" Fluffy and his friends cursed with equal frustration.

"Right," said one of the grey squirrels, "let's work out our next move."

"Yeah!" the others chorused in agreement with the grey squirrel, who appeared to be their spokesperson, if not leader.

All the grey squirrels then huddled together to form a plan.

Fluffy and his friends were also thinking about their next move.

"Right, what shall we do?" Fluffy asked. "Any ideas?"

"We could make nets out of loads of leaves if we tied their stalks together," Chalky suggested.

Fluffy thought that was an excellent idea and all the others nodded in agreement.

"Right, well let's get to work on that plan," Fluffy said.

"Yeah!" shouted his friends as they all went off to gather loads of leaves from which they would make a net capable of catching the grey squirrels.

The grey squirrels had thought of their next move. They were going to try and bowl Fluffy and friends over with an enormous mud ball they had made. It was big enough to hide behind so that Fluffy and friends would not see them until it was too late.

When Fluffy and his friends had finished making the net, which was big enough to entrap all the grey squirrels, they moved off in the direction the squirrels had been blown, carefully carrying the net between them.

After ten minutes, the grey squirrels saw Fluffy and friends approaching and pushed the mud ball towards them.

Fluffy and his friends made a run for it, holding onto their leaf net. When they had run far enough away from immediate danger, they stopped to consider their options.

"Well, that didn't work," said Fluffy, disappointed with all their failed attempts so far.

"No," his friends replied, also downcast.

The grey squirrels were celebrating.

"Yeah! We've got them away from us!" their spokesman shouted with much joy.

But Fluffy and his friends were not so easily defeated and had come up with another plan.

"Right," Fluffy said. "Let's go back at them; we'll use our net to capture the mud ball and take it off them."

"Yeah!" They all agreed and, carrying the net, went back to where the grey squirrels were. They threw the net over the mud ball to catch it and then dragged it away from the squirrels.

The grey squirrels ran after the mud ball and grabbed it. Fluffy and friends would not let go and there was a tussle to hold on to it. Suddenly, the leaf net snapped under the strain and the mud ball rolled free, killing some of the grey squirrels as it gathered speed. The rest of the grey squirrels ran away, screaming with fear.

"Excellent," said Fluffy to his friends. "Result."

The grey squirrels continued to run until they were out of sight of Fluffy and his friends.

"Well, Nutty, some of the grey squirrels who injured you and murdered your family are gone," Fluffy said. "How does that feel?"

Nutty nodded. "Pretty good."

Fluffy smiled with satisfaction. "Right, now did anyone see where the squirrels ran screaming off to?"

No one had noticed, so Fluffy and friends went in the direction they had last seen the squirrels as they ran off, screaming.

"Can anyone see them?" Fluffy enquired.

"No."

"Okay, let's go a bit further then."

On they went, all looking out for a glimpse of the grey squirrels. They stopped again.

"Can anyone see them, now?" asked Fluffy.

"No."

"We'll continue," Fluffy said. Those grey squirrels have to be somewhere."

"Yeah!"

"I still can't see them," Fluffy said after another half hour.

"Nor can I," Foley added.

Tired, but determined, Fluffy and friends continued forward. Then Fluffy saw a movement through the trees. The grey squirrels were lying low.

"There they are," whispered Fluffy. "Come on, we'll take them by surprise."

But someone trod on a dry twig and the grey squirrels heard it snap.

"They're coming back at us," said their spokesman. "I can see them."

Fluffy and his friends advanced in an attempt to attack the grey squirrels, but the squirrels managed to block their efforts.

"Couldn't get us this time," one of them jeered.

"We will," Fluffy assured him. "We're not done yet."

Then Fluffy and friends surged forward and laid into the grey squirrels.

"See? Told you," Fluffy said.

The grey squirrels mounted a counter attack but soon gave up and ran away. Fluffy and friends chased after them but, as usual, the squirrels increased their speed and got away. Fluffy and friends continued to chase the grey squirrels until they came to a lake. The sight of all that water alarmed the squirrels and they veered off in another direction. This gave Fluffy an idea and he raised his paws, telling his friends to stop for a moment. He drew his friends together and whispered to them what was on his mind.

Fluffy and his friends then skirted the bank of the lake. They turned round and began taunting the grey squirrels.

"Hey, you're too scared to come after us! Scaredy squirrels! Cowardly squirrels!"

The squirrels turned and looked angrily at Fluffy and his friends.

"We'll show you who's scared," said the spokesman. "Come on, guys, after them!"

The grey squirrels rushed towards Fluffy and his friends at the lakeside. This was their chance to win the battle.

But just as they reached Fluffy and friends, Fluffy shouted "Split."

Fluffy and his friends instantly leapt out of the way, leaving the grey squirrels with no option but to plunge into the lake. None of them could swim and after struggling to save each other, they all drowned and were left to perish in their watery grave.

"Yeah!" shouted Fluffy and his friends, cheering and celebrating the fact that the murderous grey squirrels had gone for good. They began to chant:

"We killed the squirrels; we killed the squirrels; oh, yes, we did! Yes, we did!"

"Right," said Fluffy Rabbit. "Let's continue our journey to Animal Woods. Yeah?"

"Yeah!" his friends agreed, and still singing and chanting, they continued with their journey.

As Fluffy and his friends walked along, they noticed a rabbit entangled in some barbed wire. Unable to get free, he was in great distress.

"That fellow needs our help," Fluffy said.

"Yeah!" his friends agreed as they approached the stricken rabbit.

"We're here to help you," Fluffy told him.

The rabbit was in pain, but managed to smile weakly at Fluffy and his friends.

"Trips, let's do what we did for Nutty," Fluffy said.

Trips nodded. "Alright."

Trips and Fluffy then found some strong blades of grass and after they had released the rabbit from the barbed wire, they began to stitch up the tear wounds.

"There you go," said Fluffy, tying up the last stitch, "good as new."

The rabbit smiled kindly at Fluffy and his friends and then ran off to where he belonged.

"Right," Fluffy said, "perhaps we can continue our journey to Animal Woods now."

"Yeah!" his friends replied, anxious to be on their way.

Along the way, they came to a river. It was too deep for Fluffy to cross and Chalky would have been washed away in his ball, even though it would float. Fluffy, Nutty, Foley, Trips and Barney, carrying Chalky in his ball, all climbed onto Pip's back who carried them across the river.

"That was a good ride," they said, dismounting from Pip's back.

"Yeah, I liked that, too," Pip said.

They walked on, and after ten minutes, were faced with a steep hill.

Chalky was anxious. "Someone will have to push me up that," he said, "otherwise I will keep rolling down again."

"Don't worry, Chalky, I'll do it," Fluffy assured him.

So Fluffy pushed Chalky up the hill and the other friends followed. They soon reached the summit and stopped to catch their breath, except Chalky who had not had any climbing to do.

"Right, we've climbed the hill," Fluffy said. "Are you ready to continue our journey, my friends?"

"Yeah!" replied his friends with enthusiasm.

They continued their journey to Animal Woods.

"Smell that country air," Fluffy said, passionately.

"Yeah," answered his friends, equally passionately.

Fluffy and friends walked for some time and then realized they were hungry, so off they went in search of food.

"There are some nuts," Fluffy said, pointing to some bushes. "Let's go and eat them."

"Yeah!" his friends replied and ran over to where the nuts were. After they had eaten enough to satisfy their hunger, they continued to walk. They saw an eagle, ready to swoop on a rabbit and eat it for supper. Running towards it, they scared the eagle away.

"Don't come back," Barney warned the eagle.

"Yeah, don't come back," repeated his friends.

The rabbit smiled gratefully at Fluffy and friends and then ran away into the safety of his warren.

"Right," Fluffy said, "let's get on with our walk now."

"Yeah!" the friends agreed, and they continued on their way.

They came to a forest and walked through it, the twigs snapping beneath their feet as they moved. After walking some distance through the forest, they found a graveyard.

"Let's go in there," Fluffy suggested.

"Yeah!" his friends agreed, and they all went into the graveyard. They had a look around and Fluffy discovered a secret passage.

"Hey, look at this," he said, looking in amazement at what he'd found.

His friends came to look at the secret passage and gasped with surprise.

"Shall we enter the passage?" Fluffy asked.

"Yeah!" the friends answered enthusiastically. "Let's!"

Fluffy and friends entered the secret passage and came across the skeletal remains of some mice.

"I'm guessing they didn't get their cheese," said Foley.

They all laughed at Foley's remark, but felt embarrassed at the same time.

The friends kept walking and Fluffy wondered what they would find next.

"Yeah," the friends said, "what else will we find?"

As they walked, they saw a hole in the wall.

"Look," Fluffy said. "A hole in the wall; Let's go and see what's through there."

"Yeah, let's go through the hole," the friends replied.

"Oh my God," said Fluffy as he stepped through the hole in the wall.

Fluffy's friends looked shocked at what they were seeing. There were occult rats about to sacrifice a mouse.

"So, I'm guessing that mouse we saw didn't snuff it from lack of cheese," Foley said.

Fluffy, Nutty, Trips, Pip, Chalky and Barney all laughed, but in a restrained manner.

"Stop what you are doing right now," Fluffy said to the rats that were about to sacrifice the mouse.

The rats turned round and looked at Fluffy.

"Let's get after them," one of the rats said to the others.

All the rats kept looking at Fluffy and his friends and then began to chase after them.

"Oh no … should we? Yes, we should get involved in a fight," said Fluffy.

"Yeah, we should," said his friends, and they challenged the rats to fight against them.

The rats were ready to fight and soon they were attacking Fluffy and his friends.

"Take that, you scumbag," said Fluffy, hitting a rat.

"No, you take that," the rat said, retaliating.

"Make the leaf net fall on these animals!" shouted one of the rats.

The other rats then cast a leaf net over Fluffy and friends.

"Damn! I didn't see that coming," Fluffy said.

"Nor did I," Foley replied.

Fluffy, Foley, Trips, Nutty, Chalky, Barney and Pip all shook their heads, disappointed at being captured.

"Let's start our ritual on them," one of the rats said, with an evil grin.

"Oh boy," Fluffy said, obviously scared of what was coming.

"Yeah," his friends agreed, also frightened.

The rats then prepared to begin their ritual, which began with a screeching chant.

"My God, you're annoying," Fluffy told the rats, who were looking very uncomfortable.

"Bully for you," said another rat, smugly.

Fluffy shot him a spiteful look.

"Pass me the knife," said another rat.

"Right." Another rat handed over a knife made from a sharpened twig.

Fluffy and his friends tried moving and twisting about to try and break free from the net, but their movement was limited. Then they started biting it and after some time, had chewed enough holes in the net to be able to escape.

"Yes!" Fluffy and his friends shouted as they were released from the net's grip and ran away.

The rat with the knife tried to stab Fluffy, but he sidestepped out of the way like a rugby winger.

Fluffy and his friends ran through a tunnel, out of view of the rats. They breathed sighs of relief.

"Well, at least we're out of their sight," Fluffy said.

"Yeah," his friends agreed as they followed him along the tunnel.

Shortly, they came to a doorway and went through it.

Fluffy was horrified. "Oh my God," he uttered.

"Yeah," said his friends, also horrified at what they saw ... dead mice strung up by leaf ropes.

Fluffy and friends could hear the rats coming after them.

"I've got an idea," Fluffy said, and whispered it to his friends.

Fluffy and his friends climbed on top of each other and then Nutty, who was on top, bit through the leaf rope to free it from the ceiling. Fluffy then parted it from the dead mouse. As the rats came through the doorway, Fluffy and his friends trapped them in the rope and then tied them up with it.

"Let us go!" demanded one of the rats.

"In your dreams," Fluffy told him and ran, with his friends, through another hole in the wall, leaving the rats to struggle.

Then they came to a deep patch of raw sewage.

"Ugh ... right, let's all get up on Pip's back," Fluffy said.

"Yeah," they all agreed, scrambling onto Pip's back to avoid the raw, stinking sewage.

Pip carried all his friends across the patch of sewage and then stopped so that they could all jump off.

"That was fun," they said, as they landed on clean, dry ground.

"Not for me, it wasn't, you selfish buggers," Pip snorted.

Fluffy and friends nodded, knowing that Pip was right.

The friends walked on and came to a riddle that said, 'You must act fast if you want to last.'

"I wonder what that means?" Fluffy asked his friends.

They all shook their heads, not having a clue.

Then a load of spikes started coming down from the ceiling.

"Oh my God," Fluffy and friends exclaimed anxiously and quickly ran through a hole in the wall to avoid being spiked.

"Yeah, well, we've passed that test," Fluffy said with feeling.

"Yeah," his friends agreed, also with feeling.

They carried on walking, wondering what on earth they would find next, and in a short while, they came to another doorway which they walked through. The floor suddenly sloped downhill and they all slid down to the bottom.

"Woo-hoo, that was a hell of a ride," said Fluffy.

"Yeah," his friends agreed. "Some ride!"

They continued walking and heard a flapping sound.

"What's that?" Foley asked.

"I don't know," Fluffy answered, but I'm guessing bats."

A cloud of bats then came flying all around Fluffy and his friends.

"We can help you get out of here, if you like," one of the bats said to Fluffy.

"That would be good."

"Yeah," Fluffy's friends agreed, wholeheartedly.

"Follow us, then," the bat ordered.

With that, the bats flew off and Fluffy and his friends followed.

"So, where are you all heading for?" another bat asked Fluffy.

"Animal Woods," Fluffy answered.

"Ah, that's a nice place to be going to."

Then the bats flew ahead and Fluffy and friends continued walking until they approached a doorway.

"This is the way out," the first bat told them.

Fluffy and his friends smiled at the bats in appreciation of their help "Bye, and thank you," they said, and waved as the bats swooped off about their business.

Now they resumed their journey to Animal Woods.

"Those bats were nice," Chalky remarked to Fluffy and the other friends.

"Yeah," they all agreed. "Very nice."

They walked on until they came to a lake where some swans were swimming serenely.

"Hi," said one of the swans.

"Hi," Fluffy and friends replied.

Continuing their walk, they crossed a field of daffodils.

"Hello," said a gentle, high pitched voice, "we're daffodils."

"Foley, we all know that's you," Fluffy said.

"Damn," Foley replied.

They all smiled, except Foley, who was frustrated that his friends had seen through his pretence.

"Look," Fluffy said, pointing to the next field. "There's a field of dandelions. Are you going to pretend to be them?"

"No, but I'll blow their seed clocks in your face if you don't watch it," Foley retorted.

Fluffy laughed. "Oh well, at least then we'll know what the time is."

Foley smiled at Fluffy's joke as they carried on walking along, eventually coming to a road.

Fluffy looked both ways. "Right," he said, "we'll cross the road."

"Yeah," his friends agreed, all crossing the road together.

"Now what?" asked Trips.

"We'll walk on a bit; there may be something interesting to see."

So they walked along, seeing nothing of much interest, apart from some ducks swimming on a pond.

"Hi!" they called to the ducks.

"Quack, quack, quack qu…ack, quack, quack!" the ducks replied.

"What did they say, Fluffy?"

"I think they said, 'Good afternoon, how are you?'" Fluffy told Foley. "We'll just wave, I think."

So Fluffy and friends waved to the ducks and walked on, past the pond. Then they heard a crash of thunder.

Fluffy did not like thunder. "Oh dear," he said, "we've got to find some cover, and quickly. We shouldn't be out in the open in a thunderstorm."

"Yeah, that's right, Fluffy," his friends agreed.

As they were looking for somewhere to shelter, a flash of lightning came out of the sky, narrowly avoiding Nutty.

"Bloody hell, I was almost fried squirrel," Nutty exclaimed, and they all laughed, except Nutty, who was in shock.

Fluffy and his friends saw a bridge and ran to hide beneath it, just as another flash of lightning hit the very spot where they had been standing.

"Just as well we hid under here," Fluffy said, "or we would all be fried now."

They waited for a while, huddled together under the bridge until the lightning stopped and the storm passed over.

"Okay," Fluffy said, "let's resume our journey to Animal Woods."

"Yeah," his friends said, coming out from beneath the bridge.

They walked on, past some more daffodils, but neither Fluffy nor Foley made any sound. They all began whistling their own tunes cheerfully to themselves as they walked.

"That was fun," Fluffy said.

"Yeah," his friends agreed.

"Do you think we'll have any more adventures?" Fluffy asked.

"Yeah, bound to," the others replied.

Then they saw a lake with a huge log in the middle of it.

Fluffy pointed. "Let's go across the lake on that log," he suggested.

"Yeah," his friends agreed, and one by one they crossed to the other side.

"That was a good challenge," said Fluffy.

"Yeah," his friends all agreed with him.

Walking on, they crossed another road and then passed some trees.

"Hi there!" a woodpecker called from the top of one of the trees.

"Hi!" Fluffy and friends replied, looking up as they walked.

Then a mole popped up through the earth and squinted at them. "Hi!" he said.

"Hi!" Fluffy and friends replied.

"They're very friendly round here, aren't they?" Nutty said.

"Oh yeah," Fluffy and the others agreed. "Much nicer than those grey squirrels and scumbag rats and that nasty eagle!"

Then a fox came walking by in the opposite direction.

"Hi, folks," he said, with a wink.

"Hi," Fluffy and his friends answered.

"Another nice creature," Fluffy said.

Then they saw some kind of plants growing at the roadside.

"They look like nice plants," Fluffy said.

"Yeah," his friends agreed, and Foley went to sniff the plants.

"Mm, they smell nice, too," he observed, making the others laugh.

"Come on, let's get on with our journey," Fluffy said, patting Foley on the back.

When they had walked for a few more minutes, they caught sight of the sea in the distance.

"We must be near the beach," Fluffy said.

"Yeah," replied his friends with excitement and hurried towards the sea, to play on the beach.

"I'm an aeroplane," said Foley, running on the sand with outstretched 'wings.'

The others were all laughing at Foley, but they were just as funny, running about like mad animals.

"That was fun," Fluffy remarked.

Then they all decided to race each other along the beach and Trips won.

"Yeah, I beat you all," Trips said, very pleased with herself. "I am the champion beach runner!"

Her friends all smiled and said, "Well done, Trips."

"Now we've had some fun, let's continue walking to where we want to be," Fluffy said.

"Yeah," they all agreed as they set off again on their journey to Animal Woods.

They hadn't walked far before they came to another lake. Fluffy picked up some pebbles from the bank.

"Let's skim pebbles," he said, throwing one along the surface of the water and watching it bounce several times before disappearing.

"Yeah," his friends replied, running to gather some pebbles. They all took turns and Barney turned out to be the winner, throwing his pebble further than anyone else and with the greatest number of bounces.

"I won!" Barney shouted, raising a paw. Fluffy and the others looked at him with respect.

"You certainly did," Fluffy said. "Let's move on now."

Another field of daffodils was ahead and they walked amongst the golden flowers.

"These are very quiet daffodils," Fluffy said, sneaking a look at Foley, but Foley had nothing to say and they carried on in silence for a while, until they came to a field of cows.

Fluffy and friends looked over the gate. "Moo," Foley said, teasing them. "Mooooo!"

The cows smiled, chewing their cud, and rolling their eyes at Foley. One of them shook her head at him, but she was smiling also.

"They were friendly enough," said Fluffy as they walked on.

"Yeah," the friends agreed, "nice."

Then they saw some sheep at the other end of the field.

"Baaaah!" said one or two of the sheep, looking up at Fluffy and his friends.

"Bye," Foley answered, then turned to Fluffy. "What strange creatures; they said goodbye before we had even met properly."

Fluffy laughed. "No, Foley, they were saying Baaaah, not Bye."

"Well, what does Baaaah mean?" Foley asked.

"It means everything, that's all they ever say … it's their language."

"Blooming funny language, if you ask me," Foley retorted.

Fluffy and the others smiled at Foley and carried on walking, past the sheep, past another field, until they saw some caves.

"Look," said Fluffy, pointing. "Let's go and have a look inside those caves."

"Yeah" his friends shouted enthusiastically, and Foley forgot about the sheep.

Fluffy and friends entered the cave. It was pitch black.

"Well, there's definitely an air of mystery here," Fluffy said, his whiskers twitching in the darkness.

His friends agreed and they moved further in, where the darkness seemed more intense. Suddenly, they heard a rumbling sound behind them.

"What was that?" the friends asked, looking at Fluffy for an answer.

"I don't know," Fluffy replied, "it sounded as if it came from the entrance."

Fluffy and friends headed back towards the entrance of the cave, to find that the roof had fallen in and blocked their way out.

"Oh dear, we're stuck," Fluffy told his friends.

"Could we go and see if there's another way out?" Foley suggested.

"Yeah," agreed Fluffy and his friends, and they turned around to go and look for another way out of the dark cave.

Barney took a few steps and then stopped. "I can feel something beneath my paws," he said.

"Stand still while we have a look," Fluffy replied.

Barney stood where he was while the others tried to see what was beneath his paws. It wasn't easy in the darkness, but they saw that it was a trap door. Barney managed to pull the door open far enough for Pip to kick it wide open with his hefty iron shoes.

"Right, come on, let's go through it," Fluffy said, leading the way. His friends followed close behind him and they found themselves going down a ramp. At the end of the ramp, the friends saw a doorway.

"I wonder what's through there?" Fluffy said, intrigued.

"Let's go and see," Foley replied.

"Yeah," said the others, excited, but a little scared.

As Fluffy and his friends went through the doorway, they saw some lighted candles.

Fluffy's whiskers twitched again. "Someone must have been here recently," he observed.

The friends looked around; the candles were throwing eerie shadows on the walls.

"There's a passage ahead," Fluffy said. "Let's go there, shall we?"

"Yeah," the friends replied and, keeping close together, they went into the passage, where they saw more lit candles around the walls. Walking on, they noticed some bat droppings. Then they went through another doorway.

"The walls look like they're closing in," Foley said.

"Yeah, they do," the others agreed.

"No," said Fluffy, "actually, I think we're just drowsy."

"Yeah, could be that," his friends said.

But Fluffy and his friends then fell down. They had been knocked out. Some apes came and carried Fluffy and his friends into a room.

"We found some intruders," said one ape to another.

"Right. Put them over there," said the other ape, pointing across the room.

After a while, Fluffy and his friends woke up.

"Where are we?" Fluffy asked the apes.

"My fellow apes brought you here," said an ape who was bigger than the others.

"Why?" Fluffy wanted to know.

"Because we wanted to know why you were trespassing on our land."

"We are sorry if we were trespassing. My friends and I are just trying to get to a place called Animal Woods," Fluffy explained.

"I see. Well, then, you go straight ahead, take a left and then keep going straight ahead."

"Right, Thank you, we'll do that," Fluffy replied.

"Are there any facilities we could use?" Chalky enquired.

The big ape nodded. "Yeah, man. Do you want to use our paddling pool?"

"Yeah, cool," said Fluffy and his friends.

"Follow me, then."

Fluffy and his friends followed the ape and some more apes came along, too.

"This is exciting," Chalky said.

"Yeah," his friends agreed.

When they reached the paddling pool they all went in and played with Chalky at the shallow end.

"Have this!" Foley said, and playfully splashed his friends and the apes with water.

The apes and Fluffy and friends then retaliated and splashed Foley and they continued splashing each other until they were all drenched.

"That was fun," Fluffy declared, shaking the water from his fur.

"Yeah," his friends and the apes agreed, all shaking themselves as well.

The big ape beckoned them all to follow him.

He pointed. "There's a sauna over there, made with the help of a log fire," he explained. "We can use that to dry ourselves off."

"Right," Fluffy replied. "That would be good."

They followed the ape to the sauna and went inside.

"Wow, this feels nice," said Fluffy.

"Yeah, it does," his friends agreed, relaxing in the warmth from the log fire.

When they had dried themselves, the apes led Fluffy and his friends back to where they met them.

"We have had a good time with you," Fluffy told the apes.

The apes all smiled and waved them on their way.

"Bye," Fluffy and his friends said as they left.

"Bye," replied the apes with friendly waves.

Following the big ape's directions, they walked straight ahead, took a left turn and continued straight ahead. They were out in the open air again and on their way to Animal Woods.

"They were more nice creatures that we met," Chalky said, happily.

"Yeah," Fluffy and friends replied.

As they walked on, some birds flew over their heads.

"Hello?" they said.

Fluffy and his friends looked up. "Hi," they answered, but kept walking.

"And more nice creatures," Chalky noted.

"Yeah," they all agreed, walking past a river with a log floating along in the middle of it.

"I wonder what will be at Animal Woods?" Foley thought to himself.

"What do you all think of the journey so far?" Fluffy asked his friends. "Chalky?"

"Oh, it's been good," Chalky replied with a broad smile.

"Pip?"

"Yeah, good."

"Barney?"

"Alright, yeah."

"Foley?"

"Very good!"

"How about you, Nutty?"

"Good, yeah."

"Trips?"

"Quite good."

Fluffy nodded to his friends. "Right. I think it's been good as well."

Fluffy and his friends were wondering what other adventures lay in store before they reached their destination. As they walked, they saw some bees buzzing around, but they were obviously much too busy gathering nectar and pollen to stop and say hello. Then some seagulls flew overhead and dived down close to Fluffy and his friends.

"Hi," they shouted all at once, "Hi!" "Hi!" "Hi!"

"Hi!" Fluffy and friends shouted back.

"What do you think we shall see at Animal Woods?" Fluffy asked Foley.

"Better things than your face!" Foley replied.

They all laughed and kept walking.

"There's some more daffodils," Foley pointed out.

"And more trees ahead," Barney added.

Just past the trees, they came to a road, which they crossed, keeping close together in a group.

"I think Animal Woods lie to the right," Fluffy said.

"Yeah," his friends agreed, all bearing to their right, just as it began to rain.

"Now we're walking through the rain," Fluffy said.

"Yeah," said his friends, shaking off the raindrops, "but it's not raining much."

A rainbow appeared right in front of them and the friends stopped for a moment to look at its glorious colours.

"That's a pretty sight," Fluffy said.

"Yeah," his friends nodded, "it really is."

"Do you want to have a rest on the grass?" Fluffy asked.

"Yeah," they agreed and all sat down on the grass to rest for half an hour.

"This is relaxing," Fluffy said.

"Yeah, very," his friends agreed.

"Are you ready to move on now?"

"Yeah."

"How are you all feeling?" Fluffy asked his friends when they had started walking again.

"Quite hot, but passionate," Chalky said.

"Oh, right. Anybody else feeling like that?"

"We all are," his friends said as they walked on, past some flowers.

"Ooh, they look impressive," Fluffy said.

"Yeah," Chalky said, "they do."

"Very nice," Foley observed.

"Absolutely!" said Pip.

"Yeah," Barney and Nutty agreed.

"Pretty," Trips said.

After the flowers, they came to another road.

"I think we have to cross this road," Fluffy said.

"Yeah," his friends agreed and they crossed the road and carried on walking.

Then they saw some birds flying in formation.

"Look," Fluffy said, "that's clever."

His friends looked up at the birds. "Yeah," they all agreed.

Half an hour later, Fluffy and his friends encountered some ferrets.

"Hi," said the ferrets.

"Hello," Fluffy and friends replied, admiring the ferrets' slinky figures and shiny coats.

"We were thinking about searching for some conkers and having a game of football with them," suggested one of the ferrets.

"Oh, that sounds like an interesting idea," Fluffy said.

"Yeah," Fluffy's friends agreed, "very interesting."

Off they all went, Fluffy, his friends and the ferrets, to look for conkers. It wasn't easy because there weren't many of them lying around, but after about half an hour, they found a few lying beneath a huge horse chestnut tree. They picked up as many as they could manage and then Fluffy and friends and the ferrets marked out the goal ends. Then they marked out the touchlines and were ready to play.

"Right, said one of the ferrets, "We've got the pitch marked out, now we just need some supporters."

"Shall we go and search for some, then?" Fluffy asked.

"Yes, let's do that," the ferret agreed, and they all went off in search of anyone who would come and act as supporters. There didn't seem to be many creatures about and they were just about to give up and make do without supporters, when they found some woodpeckers.

"Woodpeckers!" Fluffy exclaimed. "Shall we go over and speak to them?"

"Yes, come on, we'll ask them," said another ferret, going over to the woodpeckers.

"Hi," he said, "how are you?"

"Hi," replied the nearest woodpecker, "we're very well, thank you."

"That's good. We are going to have a game of football. Do you want to be our spectators?"

The woodpecker looked round at his mates and saw that they were all nodding.

"Yes," they all shouted, opening their sharp beaks.

"Right." Fluffy and friends, the ferrets and their new companions, the woodpeckers, then went off to look for some more fans. They came across some sheep.

"Oh look," said Foley, "Some more of those funny things that keeping saying goodbye."

"Sheep," Fluffy said, and it's "Baaaah, not Bye."

"Funny language, if you ask me," Foley said. "But I don't suppose it matters as long as they want to come and support one of our teams."

"Hi," said Fluffy.

"Baaaah!"

"We are going to play a game of football; would you like to come and be our fans?"

"Baaaah! Baaaah!" answered the sheep in a positive manner.

"Right, who wants to cheer my team? Whoever cheers the loudest will have that honour," said Fluffy.

"BAAAAH! BAAAAH!" the sheep cheered, making a racket.

The woodpeckers flew off to some nearby tall beech trees and began hammering them with all their might. The noise they made was louder than the sheep cheering.

"So, the woodpeckers will be cheering our team," Fluffy decided.

"Yeah," his friends agreed, and they and Fluffy went back to the football pitch with the ferrets, the woodpeckers and the sheep.

"Let's line up in our positions," said a ferret.

"Yeah, let's," Fluffy replied. "Come on, who's going to be in goal?"

The ferrets found their positions and so did Fluffy and his friends and the woodpeckers gathered behind Fluffy's goal, while the sheep herded themselves behind the ferrets' goal.

"We haven't got a referee," said one of the ferrets.

"That's because we're playing freestyle," Fluffy explained.

The ferret seemed interested. "Right," he said, thoughtfully.

Fluffy kicked off, passing one of the conkers to Foley, who passed it to Chalky. Chalky, rolling the conker football along with his own ball, took a shot at the ferrets' goal. The ferret saved it.

"Oh." Chalky was disappointed.

The ferrets' goalie then bowled the ball to one of his team mates, who dribbled it forward, preparing to shoot. It was a good shot, but Barney was a good goalkeeper and saved the shot, raising his clenched paw in victory.

Barney then bowled the ball to Trips, who dribbled it down the wing, and then cross kicked it to

Fluffy. Fluffy headed it into the goal, straight past the ferret.

"YES!" shouted Fluffy.

"Well done, Fluffy," said his friends, celebrating with him before turning back to their own half.

A ferret then kicked off, passing the ball to a team mate who dribbled it forward, but was challenged by Nutty. Nutty kicked the ball to Trips. She took it down the wing and attempted to pass it to Fluffy. However, it was intercepted by a ferret, who played it to one of his colleagues. Foley challenged and won possession.

"Pass it to me," Fluffy called.

Foley passed the ball to Fluffy, who was challenged by a ferret. The ferret took the ball.

"Damn, I've lost possession," Fluffy grumbled as the ferret ran down the pitch with the ball.

The ferret pretended to continue straight ahead with the ball, but then swerved in another direction to shake Fluffy off.

"Oh no," Fluffy thought, "He's fooled me."

The ferret with possession steamed ahead with the ball at his feet.

"Risk losing to have a chance of winning," Fluffy thought, and made a firm challenge on the ferret, taking the ball and passing it to Chalky.

Chalky was not quick enough and soon lost the ball to a ferret.

"Yes, I've won the ball," the ferret boasted, but wasn't prepared for Trips, who made a feisty challenge and gained possession of the ball.

"YES!" Trips shouted, dribbling the ball forward and then passing it to Foley.

Confronted by a ferret, Foley then back-headed the ball to Trips. She passed it to Fluffy, who had a shot at the goal. The ferret jumped and saved the ball, throwing it up the pitch to a team mate.

His team mate rushed forward to get the ball, determined to keep possession, but Foley barged the ferret out of the way.

"Oh." The ferret was disappointed. "That's for being over confident," he told himself as Foley moved forward with the ball.

"Pass it to me," Fluffy shouted.

"No, pass it here," Chalky urged.

Foley decided to pass the ball to Chalky, who then moved forward, dribbling the ball before shooting at the goal. It was a brilliant, well-timed shot, but the ferret dived to save it.

"I saved it! Yes, I saved it!" the ferret said to himself and then bowled the ball to a team mate.

The team mate ran forward with the ball, ready to shoot, but Foley swiftly moved in and won the ball from him, attempting to pass it to Fluffy.

Before Fluffy could take the pass, another ferret intercepted the ball and ran forward with it.

Foley shook his head. "Bugger!"

Fluffy thought he would win the ball back from the ferret and ran in to tackle him, winning the ball from him, but immediately losing it again as the ferret counter tackled.

"Yes! I've won the ball," sang the ferret, moving forward and unleashing a shot at goal.

Barney easily reached the ball and turned it wide of the goalpost and out of play.

"Yes! That was an awesome save," Barney told himself as a ferret prepared to take the corner kick.

When the ferret took the corner kick, Barney shot out of his goal and took possession of the ball.

"Pass it here!" Fluffy shouted.

Barney threw the ball down the pitch to Fluffy, who dribbled it forward.

Foley ran parallel to Fluffy. "Pass it here," he shouted.

As Fluffy passed the ball across to Fluffy, a ferret rushed in and intercepted.

"Oh no," groaned Foley.

Trips then mounted a fierce challenge on the ferret and won the ball.

"Yes!" Trips was pleased with herself for winning the ball and moved forward with it.

"Pass it here!" Fluffy shouted to her.

"No," Chalky said, "pass it here."

Trips decided to pass the ball to Chalky.

Chalky thought he was good at dribbling and moved forward confidently, passing the ball accurately to Fluffy.

"I'm going to take the ball off that rabbit," thought one of the ferrets, going in for a tackle. He took the ball from Fluffy and then had it taken from him by Chalky, who passed it to Trips.

Trips thought she would have a long shot at goal and kicked the ball down the pitch to the opposing goal.

The ferret in goal leapt high in the air and saved the ball.

"Oh no," Trips said. She had been certain that she was going to score.

The ferrets had possession and ran up the pitch, passing the ball between them, but Fluffy put a spurt on and managed to get possession of the ball again.

"Pass it to me," Foley shouted and as Fluffy tried to pass the ball, a ferret intercepted.

"Yes, I've won," the ferret thought and moved the ball forward, trying to dodge Chalky, who was rolling to and fro in front of the ferret.

"I'm going to win this battle," Chalky thought and managed to take the ball from the ferret and pass it to Fluffy. "Yes," Chalky said to himself, "that was an impressive pass."

"Thanks, Chalky," Fluffy said and dribbled the ball forward.

"Pass it to me!" Trips shouted.

Fluffy pretended to have a go at passing the ball to Trips and fooled the opposing ferret. Fluffy took a shot at the ferrets' goal but the keeper rushed out and caught the ball.

"I'll throw it out," the goalkeeper thought.

"Pass it to me!" shouted one of the ferrets.

"No, to me!" another one insisted.

The goalkeeper threw the ball to the nearest ferret, who dribbled it forward, but was confronted by Fluffy.

Fluffy quickly won the ball off the ferret. "Yes!" he thought, and passed it to Chalky.

Chalky thought he would move the ball forward, but a ferret challenged him. "No, you don't," Chalky thought, rolling as fast as he could and pushing the ball ahead of him. "Keep rolling!"

"I'll try and tackle him," thought the ferret.

"I won't let him have the ball," thought Chalky.

Another ferret then came in and kicked the ball away from Chalky.

"Oh no, I've lost it," Chalky groaned and tried to win the ball back.

The ferret in possession avoided him. "Should I pass or keep moving forward?" he thought. Looking around, he decided there would be no advantage in passing. "I'll keep moving forward," he decided.

Foley then intercepted and won the ball from the ferret. The ferret immediately took the ball back and passed it to a colleague, who saw an opening and had a shot at the goal, putting it past Barney to equalise.

"YES! One all," the ferret shouted in celebration. All his team mates gathered round him to celebrate as well and the sheep cheered on the ferrets, making a racket with their noisy baaa-ing.

Fluffy then kicked the ball to Foley.

"Pass it to me," Chalky shouted.

"Yeah," Foley answered, passing the ball to Chalky.

The woodpeckers hammered the tree trunks to show Chalky their support, as he rolled the ball forward.

Then a ferret ran in and won the ball off him.

"To me!" shouted another ferret.

"No, me," said another, running in.

"Thanks," said the one who took possession and moved forward.

"Pass it back to me," urged the one who had just passed it.

But the ferret with possession ignored him and kept moving with the ball.

"I'm going to take the ball off you," Foley warned and ran towards the ferret to try and take possession.

However, the ferret was too fast and ran rings around Foley.

"Oh." Foley was disappointed that he lost the challenge.

The ferret in possession thought he would have a shot at goal, but Barney saved it.

"Throw it to me!" Foley shouted.

"No, to me," said Chalky.

Barney threw the ball to Foley who moved forward with it.

Trips ran alongside. "Pass it to me!" she shouted.

"Pass it to me!" Fluffy shouted at the same time.

Foley ignored them both and decided to keep moving forward. As he approached the goal, he kicked the ball with all his might, hoping to score, but his shot was blocked by a ferret.

The sheep then began to cheer the ferrets on and the ferret who blocked Foley's shot took the ball away from his own goal, but soon lost it to Fluffy.

"Pass it to me!" yelled Chalky.

"No, to me," Trips said.

As Fluffy moved forward, Chalky decided to run alongside him. Fluffy then made a one-two pass between Chalky and himself. "I'll have a crack at goal," he thought and kicked the ball straight at the opposition goal.

The ferret dived forward and saved the ball and the sheep began their baaa-ing cheers again.

"I'll throw it to my nearest colleague," the ferret thought, and did just that.

The nearest ferret took the throw and moved forward with the ball, but Fluffy came in and took possession. The woodpeckers hammered the tree trunks to cheer that winning challenge.

"Pass it to me," Foley said.

Fluffy passed it to Foley who moved forward, dribbling the ball.

A ferret then tackled Foley and won the ball from him, causing the sheep to cheer the tackle.

The ferret gave the supporting sheep a look of appreciation.

"Pass it to me!" shouted a ferret, but was ignored as the one in possession continued to move forward.

"I'll remove him from the ball," Foley thought and went in to tackle the ferret, winning the ball from him,

The woodpeckers cheered Foley's challenge and watched as he moved forward. He was just about to pass the ball when the same ferret tackled him and won the ball back.

The sheep cheered at that challenge, but went quiet when Fluffy tackled and again won the ball.

"Yes!" Fluffy shouted.

"Yes!" the woodpeckers shouted, in between hammering the tree with their long beaks.

Fluffy moved forward with the ball and played a one-two pass with Nutty.

"Go on!" Chalky shouted.

Fluffy had a shot at the goal, but the ferret dived to the ball and put it out of play for a corner kick to Fluffy's team.

Foley said he would take it and went and kicked it to Fluffy.

However, Fluffy kicked it high and wide of the goal.

"Shame on me," he thought. "That would have been poor, even for a Newcastle Falcon's kick."

The ferret in goal took the goal kick, sending the ball to the other end of the pitch. One of his colleagues tried to get on the end of the ball, but Barney came forward and punched it well away from the goal mouth and the ferret.

Fluffy then thought he would get on the end of it and succeeded, but a ferret intercepted as he moved forward and won the ball.

"Pass it to me!" shouted another ferret as the sheep cheered.

"No, to me," another ferret said.

But the ferret in possession ignored them both and kept moving forward.

"I'll tackle him," thought Fluffy, and ran in, winning the ball from the ferret.

The woodpeckers cheered the tackle, but then Fluffy was challenged by another ferret and had the ball removed from him.

"Damn!" he said, exasperated.

The sheep were cheering the ferret, who took the ball forward and passed it to a colleague.

Foley was ready for the ferret's pass. "I'll win this one," he thought and challenged. He won the ball, causing the woodpeckers to cheer. He moved forward, thinking he would beat his opponent, and started weaving the ball around the ferret.

"I'll remove the ball from him," thought the ferret, and then took the ball from Foley.

Foley then fought back, successfully removing the ball from the ferret and moving forward. However, another ferret came and won the ball from him.

"NO!" Foley shouted.

"YES!" the ferret replied and then moved forward. "I'll beat all the opponents," he thought, and did exactly that.

The sheep cheered, celebrating a good show of play by the ferret.

"Pass it to me," shouted another ferret.

Chalky was watching the ball. "I'll tackle in a moment," he thought.

The ferret in possession passed the ball to his colleague, who then tried a long shot to Barney's goal.

The sheep cheered as the ferret took the shot and the woodpeckers cheered even louder when Barney saved it. Barney threw the ball to Chalky, who stopped it and then rolled forward with it.

The woodpeckers went wild with delight as Chalky got away with the ball and looked certain to score. But then a ferret made a late tackle and won the ball from him.

"Yes!" said the ferret, dribbling the ball to safety.

"Pass it to me!" shouted another ferret.

"No, to me!" Trips shouted, fooling the ferret and easily taking the ball from him.

The woodpeckers were enjoying this and cheered as Trips took the ball forward.

"Huh, I'll tackle her," the duped ferret said to himself and soon won the ball back.

"Play it to me," another ferret said and took the pass. "Yes, I'm on the ball!" he sang, moving forward.

Foley was ready for him and went toe to toe with the ferret, removing the ball from him.

"YES!" Foley shouted as the woodpeckers' excitement mounted.

Foley played a one to one passing movement with Trips, who then passed the ball to Fluffy. Fluffy tried to shoot but a ferret threw himself in the way and won the ball.

The ferret moved forward, passing the ball to a colleague, but Foley intercepted it, gaining possession.

"Yes!" Foley moved forward, passed the ball to Trips, who kept good control of the ball and the woodpeckers cheered her play until a ferret tackled and won the ball. Trips quickly recovered and won the ball back.

The woodpeckers were hammering like crazy, cheering her on as she played the ball to Fluffy.

"Time's up; next goal wins it!" said one of the woodpeckers to Fluffy.

"Right," Fluffy said, shooting at the goal, but again kicked the ball straight to a ferret.

The ferret moved forward and took a shot at the goal. The ball whizzed past Barney's outstretched paws to make the score 2-1 to the ferrets, winning the game for them against Fluffy and friends.

"YES!" shouted the victorious ferret and the sheep made a racket, baaa-ing with delight at their teams' success. The woodpeckers were disappointed, but hammered briefly to congratulate the winners.

Well done," Fluffy said to the ferrets, "and thanks for your support," he said to the woodpeckers. Fluffy and friends saluted the woodpeckers in a gesture of appreciation and the ferrets did likewise to the sheep.

"We're off now," Fluffy told the ferrets, "to Animal Woods. Thanks for the game. Goodbye."

"That's okay, bye," the ferrets replied.

Fluffy and friends waved farewell to the ferrets and resumed their journey to Animal Woods.

That was an impressive game of football," Fluffy said as they walked.

"Yeah," his friends agreed.

As they continued their journey, it began to rain.

"Ah, we need to battle the elements now," Fluffy remarked.

"Yeah," Foley agreed and started to hum 'Singing in the Rain.'

His friends smiled and then the sun peeped out from a cloud and a rainbow appeared, stretching from one hill to another.

"Wow, that's impressive," Fluffy declared.

His friends agree. "Yeah," they murmured, staring at its beauty before them.

On they walked, along a road bordered by a patch of grass. They continued along there for about half an hour, until they came to a place called Ambleside.

"Shall we stop and see what's here?" Fluffy asked.

"Yeah," his friends agreed, and they walked on, passing beneath an archway.

Chalky was impressed. "That's artistic," he observed.

"Yeah," his friends agreed.

Fluffy and his friends kept walking, passing through villages, until they came to a pasture.

"Look, there are some more sheep," Fluffy pointed out and he and his friends waved to the sheep.

The sheep stopped munching for a moment to wave back and then carried on grazing.

After walking for a while, they came to a place called Windermere.

"What a beautiful lake," Fluffy said.

"Yeah," Barney agreed, "and the mountains are impressive."

"A bit like hooters," said Foley, making the others laughed as they walked on.

They met a car and some people, and after a while, they found themselves approaching a place called High Close, going down a hill called Dead Man's Drop.

"That was fun," Fluffy said.

"Yeah, it was," said Foley, and the others agreed.

As Fluffy and his friends kept walking, a cool breeze blew up, making them shiver.

"Right," said Fluffy, "we need to believe more in our hearts."

"Yeah, we do," his friends agreed and, believing more in their hearts, they battled through the breeze.

"We're doing it," Fluffy said.

"Yeah," his friends agreed, "believing more in our hearts."

As they walked on, some people drove past in cars and waved at them.

Fluffy and his friends waved back.

"They seemed nice," Fluffy said.

"Yeah, they did," his friends agreed.

Chalky thought Fluffy had something on his mind and asked him what it was.

"As a matter of fact," Fluffy replied, "I'm thinking about playing in Animal Woods."

"That's good. I'm thinking about rolling around in there, as well.

"I am going to gallop around when we get to Animal Woods," Pip said, rolling his big brown eyes.

"I shall have a play fight with Foley," Barney declared.

"We'll have one right now," said Foley and he and Barney began play fighting.

"I'll run around like crazy," Trips said.

"I think I shall hunt for some nuts," added Nutty.

On they walked, towards Animal Woods.

"How excited are you?" Fluffy asked.

"Very excited," his friends replied, and they all did a skip and a jump as they walked.

"That was fun," said Fluffy.

"Yeah," they all agreed, as they passed some fields and trees. They loved the smell of them and breathed in deeply.

Fluffy closed his eyes, "Refreshing."

"Yeah," his friends agreed as some people in a horse and cart went past them.

"Hi," said the people in the cart.

"Hello," Fluffy and his friends replied.

"They were good to us," Foley said.

"Yeah, they were," Fluffy replied.

His friends nodded in agreement as they continued their journey to Animal Woods.

"What are we going to do next?" Foley asked.

"Keep on walking," Fluffy replied.

As they walked, some birds flew overhead.

"Good day," said the birds, looking down at them.

"Hi," replied Fluffy and friends, looking up and waving as they continued on their journey.

They came to a place called Keswick.

"Look, there's a park," Fluffy said.

"Let's go through it," suggested Foley.

"Yeah," the others replied as they made for the entrance gates.

"Shall we run around madly?" Fluffy asked his friends.

"Yeah, let's do that!" his friends replied, and they all ran round in circles until they were breathless.

"Phew!" Fluffy exclaimed, "That was fun."

"Yeah," his friends agreed, and when they had their breath back, they resumed their journey to Animal Woods.

"What do you make of the journey so far?" Fluffy asked Foley.

"It's alright," Foley answered.

"It's good to me," Trips added.

"It's been impressive to me," Pip said.

"Spot on for me," from Nutty.

"And fine for me," Chalky piped up.

"Yeah, fine for me as well," Barney agreed.

"And how are your feet?" Fluffy asked as they walked on.

"Well, a bit sore," Foley replied.

"Yeah, ours are the same," the others agreed, but they all kept walking.

Some traffic passed them on the road and then they saw a meadow full of wild flowers.

"They look impressive," Foley observed.

"Fresh, too," Barney said with approval.

"Yeah, beautiful," the others agreed as they walked past.

Then they came to a farm where a sheepdog was sitting on guard, looking bored.

"Hey!" he called out. "I challenge you lot to a race."

"Alright," Fluffy said.

"Yeah," his friends agreed, going towards the sheepdog.

"Okay, are you ready to race?" he asked them.

"Yeah, we're ready," the friends replied.

"Right, three … two … one … GO!"

The sheepdog, Fluffy and his friends then raced against each other. The sheepdog ran fast and appeared to be winning, but then Trips came through and won the race.

"Well done," said the sheepdog, his tongue hanging out.

"Thanks," Trips said with a smile.

"Thanks for the race," Fluffy said. "Now we must be on our way."

"Yeah," his friends said, nodding agreement.

"Okay, bye then," said the sheepdog.

"Bye!"

They moved on, waving to the sheepdog, who had been pleased to relieve his boredom for a few minutes.

"That was fun," Fluffy said.

"Yeah," Foley agreed.

They walked for quite a while and then came to Penrith.

"This is a nice place," Fluffy said. "Let's walk by those shops."

"Yeah," his friends agreed and they walked past the shops, then carried straight on until they came to Carlisle.

"Shall we visit Carlisle Castle?" Fluffy asked his friends.

"Yeah," they replied, heading for the castle. Once inside, they looked around.

"This is old," said Fluffy. "Archaic, in fact."

"Yeah," his friends agreed as they walked through together.

"Let's go and see Brunton Park Football Stadium," Fluffy said when they came out of the castle.

"Yeah," his friends agreed, "let's do that." They found their way to the home of Carlisle United Football Club.

"It's a football stadium," Barney observed.

"No!" Foley said. "Never!"

They all laughed. Fluffy said, "Let's keep moving," and they continued walking amongst other pedestrians as cars passed them.

"More people around here," Fluffy said.

"Yeah," his friends agreed as they kept on the move.

"This is good, isn't it?" Fluffy said. "We're gradually making our way to Animal Woods."

"Yeah," they all agreed.

A bit further along, they passed a black Labrador.

"Hi," said Fluffy and his friends as they passed.

"Hi. My name's Orton," the Labrador replied, wagging his tail and looking at Barney with interest.

"Mine's Barney. Bye Orton."

"Bye," Orton replied, watching Fluffy and friends walking away from him.

"He was alright," Foley said, "for a dog."

"Yeah," replied Fluffy and the others. "He was."

A while later, they came to Newcastle.

"Here we are, in the town," Fluffy said. "Shall we explore it?"

"Yeah," his friends replied, ready to explore the town. After that, they went to a place called Gosforth. Walking down Gosforth High Street, they came to a place called the Regent Centre. They saw a metro station.

"Hey, I wonder what's in there?" Foley said.

"Lots of people and metro trains," Fluffy replied, making a train movement with his paws.

"Right."

The friends kept walking, and after a while, came to Fawdon metro station.

"Another one," Fluffy said, pointing to it.

"Yeah."

Then they came to Fawdon Bridge and walked over it.

"That's a train track," Fluffy told his friends.

"Yeah, we know it is," his friends replied.

Walking on, they passed Kingston Park and went on to Kenton.

"What's this place?" Barney asked, sniffing the air.

"The sign says Kenton," Foley told him.

"Oh. Silly me for not seeing that," Barney laughed.

Then they were heading for the Town Moor.

"The Town Moor," Fluffy said. "It says the Hoppings Fairground is coming soon."

"Groovy," said Foley.

Fluffy and his friends kept moving. Then they came to a place called Barrack Road, Fenham, and Newcastle. Then came Exhibition Park, and then Jesmond.

"There's nothing worthwhile here," Fluffy said.

"Yeah, I bet these houses are overpriced," Foley said, looking around him.

Fluffy and the others smiled at his remark and they all carried on walking into Newcastle City Centre.

They were walking by the side of a motorway. Fluffy said, "We're taking a risk; a motorist might spin out of control and crash into us!"

His friends laughed.

"We'd better keep moving," Fluffy told them.

They carried on walking while cars and trucks rushed past them and, eventually, they reached Northumberland.

"We're in Northumbria," Fluffy told his friends.

"Yeah. Are we stopping here?" Foley asked.

"No, we'll keep walking," Fluffy replied and they walked on until they came to a place called Morpeth.

"Let's go into the town centre," Fluffy suggested.

"Alright. Shall we go and play in the park?" asked Barney.

"Yeah, let's go and play," the friends agreed, and went to the park, where they had a lot of fun.

"That was spot on. Let's move on now," Fluffy said.

"Okay," his friends agreed and they resumed their journey once more.

"What did you think of the park?" Fluffy asked them as they walked.

"Yeah, it was alright," his friends agreed.

"I thought so, too," Fluffy said.

Near a roundabout, next to the train station, they came to Morpeth Cenotaph.

"Look," Fluffy said, "there are all the names of the fallen brave."

His friends nodded and stood for a moment to look at the names carved into the memorial. They walked along a path beside the road where there were some benches, as well as a grassy bank. The bank looked quite steep.

"Should we roll down there?" Fluffy asked his friends.

"Yeah!"

Fluffy and his friends threw themselves to the ground and rolled down the grassy bank, shouting and laughing as they went.

"This is thrilling!" Fluffy declared.

"Yeah," his friends agreed, "very thrilling."

They got to their feet, dusted themselves down and then continued with their walk.

"That was a good roll, wasn't it?" Fluffy said.

"Yeah, great," his friends agreed.

"Rock and roll," Foley added, making the others laugh.

"There's a path," Fluffy said as they walked, and he led them down it, whistling as they went.

"This is good," Fluffy said.

"Yeah," Trips replied. "I wonder where it leads to?"

As they came to the end of the path, they saw a golf course ahead of them.

"Fore!" Foley shouted, pretending to take a shot down the course.

Fluffy and the others laughed. "You're still on form, I see," Fluffy remarked.

Foley smiled. "Thanks."

They carried on walking. "I wonder what we'll see next," Fluffy said.

Before long they passed a council building. There was a drain nearby.

"Hello," said a rat, peering up at them from the bottom of the drain.

"Hi," replied Fluffy and friends.

The rat twitched his whiskers. "Where are you going?"

"Animal Woods," Fluffy told him.

"Okay. Bye!"

"Bye," replied Fluffy and his friends.

The next place they came to was a caravan park.

"Are we going in there?" Barney asked.

"No," said Fluffy, "we are going to keep on walking."

"Oh." Barney looked disappointed.

"How far do you think we have walked?" Foley asked Fluffy.

"Longer than we walked an hour ago," Fluffy answered, making Foley and the others laugh. "Look, there's a stray cat; let's stop and talk to him."

"Yeah," his friends replied. "Hi!"

"Hi," said the cat. "My name's Ross. Whereabouts are you going?"

"Animal Woods," they told him.

"Alright. Will there be chicks there?" Ross asked.

"Maybe there could be female birds," Fluffy replied.

His friends and Ross smiled.

"Where were you going?" Fluffy asked him.

"Oh, just out having a walk."

"Okay. Well, we'll be on our way," said Fluffy.

"Bye," said Ross.

"Goodbye, take care," Fluffy replied.

"Yeah," said his friends, "Bye!"

Ross then continued his walk and Fluffy and friends continued theirs.

"That was a nice cat we met," Fluffy said.

"Yeah, he was a nice cat," his friends agreed as they walked past some fields.

"More fields," Fluffy said. "What do you think we shall see next?"

"I don't know," Foley said. "Let's keep walking and find out."

"How can we improve this journey? Any ideas?"

"Let's have a race," Foley suggested.

"Yeah," the others agreed, and got into position, ready for the off.

Fluffy pointed ahead. "Right, first one past that big oak tree is the winner. Get ready, get set … GO!"

They all ran as fast as they could, but Fluffy was the clear winner.

"I won!" he said.

"Well done," said his friends.

"Thanks. That was an impressive race."

"Should we keep on walking?" Foley asked.

"Yeah, we keep on walking."

When they came to a fairly high hedge, Foley jumped level with the top of it.

"Look at me," he said, jumping again.

His friends just smiled at him and they continued moving forward on their journey.

"I feel excited," Fluffy said.

"Ditto," replied his friends.

As they walked on, they came to a motorway bridge.

"There's a footpath," Fluffy said.

"Yeah," the others agreed.

"Do you want to walk along it?"

"Yeah."

Fluffy and his friends walked along the footpath. "This is nice," Fluffy remarked.

"It is," his friends agreed.

They continued walking and came to a train station.

"There's a train station," Fluffy pointed out.

"Yeah. Shall we go in and have a look round?" Foley suggested.

"Yeah," Fluffy and the others agreed and went to look round the station.

"Let's walk along the platform," Fluffy suggested.

"They walked along the platform.

"What do you want to do now?" Fluffy asked.

"Well, there's nothing else here, so we might as well go," Foley replied.

They all agreed and left the station.

"That was good," Fluffy said.

"Yeah," his friends agreed.

"Let's walk a bit further."

They walked along by a road. Some birds were flying overhead.

"Hi," said the birds.

"Hi," Fluffy and his friends answered.

"Where are you going?" asked one of the birds.

"We're going to Animal Woods," Fluffy replied.

"Okay. Bye bye."

"Bye," said Fluffy and his friends.

"Should we keep walking?" Foley asked.

"Yeah," the others answered and as they carried on walking, some cars passed them and a lorry containing people.

"Let's wave," Fluffy said.

"Okay," his friends agreed, and began to wave at the drivers and passengers.

They walked on for a while and then Fluffy asked them if they wanted to keep on walking.

"Yeah," his friends answered.

"Is the journey still okay?" Fluffy then asked.

"Yeah, it is," Foley replied.

"It is," Pip agreed.

"Yeah, it's okay," said Chalky.

"Yes," Trips answered.

"It's okay," Barney said.

"I agree with everybody," Nutty said.

"That's good," Fluffy said. "We'll carry on with it, then."

A bit further on they came to a village shop.

The shop owner waved to them. "Hi," he said.

"Hi," Fluffy and friends replied.

"He was nice," Fluffy commented, when they had passed the shop.

"Yeah," the others agreed as they continued to walk. Then they saw some birds stealing nuts from some other birds.

"Look at that!" Fluffy exclaimed. "Let's go and help the birds who are being robbed."

"Okay," his friends agreed and they all went towards the thieving birds and dived on them.

"You're nicked," Foley told the bird he had dived on.

The robbed birds quickly retrieved their nuts from the thieving birds.

"Thanks for helping us," one of the birds shouted to Fluffy and his friends.

"Yes, thank you," the other robbed birds said, smiling with appreciation. As they flew off with their nuts, they waved their wings at Fluffy and his friends.

Fluffy and friends waved back.

"They were alright," Fluffy said.

"Yeah, they were," the others agreed as they continued to walk.

"How are you feeling?" Fluffy asked his friends.

"Quite happy," Foley replied.

"I'm excited," Trips said.

"Tired, but I'll keep going," Barney said.

"Happy," said Pip.

Chalky said he was alright.

"I'm fine," Nutty said.

As they walked, they saw a hedgehog by the side of the road.

"Make sure you don't get squashed," Foley said.

"Oh yeah, I can make sure I don't become road kill," the hedgehog replied. "Where are you lot going?"

"Animal Woods."

"Okay. Bye, then."

"Bye."

Fluffy and his friends left the hedgehog behind and continued their march to Animal Woods.

Foley started humming a Keane song.

"Stop for a minute," Fluffy said and he and his friends smiled at Foley as they all carried on moving forward.

They were all quite smug as they walked and then they fell into a hole in the ground, hitting the bottom with a thud.

"This is no Alice's Wonderland," Foley said.

"Nah … there's no weird bunnies, unless you count Fluffy!" Trips joked.

"I heard that," Fluffy said.

His friends giggled.

"Shall we explore this place?" Fluffy asked.

"Yeah," his friends agreed and they all set off to explore the hole they had fallen into.

"Wonder what we'll find?" Fluffy said.

"Yeah," the others said.

Fluffy and his friends then went down some mud steps made by animals, judging by the paw prints in the mud. They carried on walking downstairs until they reached the bottom, where they found a load of badgers watching them.

"What are you doing in our hole?" asked one of the badgers.

"We fell into it," Fluffy explained.

"Oh, right. Well, you must have been stupid," said the badger.

"I prefer dumb, but whatever," Fluffy replied.

"Are you going to tell us how to get out?" Foley asked.

"I'll tell you how to get out when each of you has had a fight with each of us."

"Okay," Foley and the others agreed.

"Right. I want you to get into rival pairs and imagine a new move each, and then make a new sport."

Fluffy and his friends formed rival pairs with the badgers.

"My name's Baby and my move is leaping into the air," said one of the badgers.

"Hi, Baby. My name's Foley and my move is crashing into you and trying to knock you down."

"Okay," Baby said. "So our sport can be called Leap Crashing."

"Yeah, right," Foley agreed.

Fluffy introduced himself to a badger. "I'm Fluffy and my move's running diagonally."

"Hi, Fluffy," the badger replied. "My name's Ben and my move is jumping in the air to see who can jump the highest, so we can be Angle Jumping."

"Okay."

"Hi, I'm Jim and my move's hopping along."

"Hi, Jim. I'm Trips and my move is throwing myself forward and seeing who can get further forward, so our sport can be called Hop Throwing."

Jim agreed.

The others were introducing themselves.

"Hi there, my name's Jack and my move is shoving, so whoever is moved backwards first loses."

"Hi. I'm called Chalky and my move is rolling in my ball, so our sport can be Roll Shoving."

"Hi, my name's Bobby and my move is diving on the floor and whoever hits it first wins a point."

"Hi, my name's Nutty and my move is running around in a circle, so our sport will be called circle diving."

"Hiya, my name's Stevie and my move is spinning round in a circle."

"Oh, I see. I'm Barney and my move is clapping my paws together, so our sport will be Spin Clapping.

"Hi, I'm John and my move is jumping as fast as can be."

"Hi, my name's Pip and my move is galloping along, so our sport can be Gallop Fast Jumping."

"Right. Foley and I will play Leap Crashing in a best of nine contests," Baby said. "Are you ready, Foley?"

"Ready."

Foley and Baby then leapt in the air and crashed into each other, but neither of them was knocked to the ground.

"That's the first point drawn," Baby said.

Foley agreed.

Baby and Foley leapt at each other again, and this time, Foley knocked Baby to the floor.

"Yeah, I won that point," Foley said.

Baby agreed.

They leapt at each other again; this time Baby knocked Foley down.

"One all," Baby declared.

"Let's continue," Foley said, anxious to beat his opponent.

Again they threw themselves at each other, with Baby knocking Foley to the ground again.

"Yeah, I'm ahead," Baby said.

They leapt at each other again and once more Foley was knocked down. Then Baby knocked him down again in the sixth bout.

"I'm still ahead," Baby asserted.

They leapt at each other again and Foley knocked Baby down.

"I'm only three-two down now," Foley said.

"Okay," Baby said, and knocked Foley down again in the next bout.

"Yay, I'm two ahead now!"

Next time they leapt at each other, Foley used more force and knocked Baby to the ground.

"Yes! Only four-three," Foley declared.

Again they leapt at each other and Baby put Foley on the ground.

"I win the Leap Crashing contest!" Baby exclaimed.

"Yeah, well done, Baby," said Foley.

"Right, now Fluffy and I will play Angle Jumping in a best of nine contest," Ben announced. "Are you ready, Fluffy?"

"Yes!"

Fluffy and Ben then ran diagonally at each other, before jumping in the air, reaching up.

Ben jumped the highest. "Yeah, I win," he said.

Then they ran at each other again and jumped in the air, reaching up. Fluffy jumped the highest and levelled the score.

"Yeah," Fluffy said. My turn to win."

The two of them then ran at a tilted angle, jumped in the air and reached up. Ben was the highest jumper.

"Two-one to me!" he said.

Fluffy nodded, ready for the next angle jump.

They ran at a Dutch angle and jumped in the air, reaching for the sky. This time, Fluffy won.

"Level now, two all," he said.

They ran again at another angle, jumping in the air and reaching up. Ben jumped marginally higher than Fluffy.

"Yes, three two to me!" said Ben

Again, they ran at each other diagonally, jumping and then reaching upwards. Fluffy made it this time.

He nodded. "Three all now, Ben."

"Not for long," Ben replied. "Come on, next one."

They turned away from each other, then ran in at an angle, jumped in the air and reached up as high as they could. Fluffy jumped highest again.

"Yes. Four-three now," he said, excited to be in the lead.

Fluffy and Ben repeated the running and jumping in the air, with Ben jumping higher this time, levelling the score again.

"Four all," he said.

"The next one will be the decider," Fluffy said. "Are you ready?"

"I'm ready," Ben replied.

Running at an angle, they both made a big effort and jumped as high as they could, reaching upwards. Fluffy was the winner.

"Yes," he shouted. "I'm the winner of Angle Jumping!"

"You are, Fluffy. Well done," said Ben.

"Right. Trips and I will play Hop Throwing now," said Jim. "Ready, Trips?"

Trips nodded and then she and Jim hopped along and then threw themselves forward. Trips landed in front of Jim.

"Yes, I am furthest forward," Trips said.

"Okay," Jim agreed.

They hopped along again, throwing themselves forward and Trips won again.

"Yes, two-nil," Trips said.

"Yeah, it is," Jim agreed.

They hopped along as before, throwing themselves forward and this time Jim landed in front of Trips.

"Yes!" Jim said. "I'm only one behind now."

Again they hopped along, throwing themselves forward and Jim won again.

"I've come back," he said, getting ready for the next hop throw.

Once more, they hopped along, throwing themselves forward and Trips managed to land ahead of Jim.

"Yes!" Trips said. "Three-two now."

After the next hop jump, the score was level again at three all.

They hopped along and threw themselves forward, Jim trying very hard to equalise, but Trips managed to beat him.

"No need to go again," Trips said. "I've won the Hop Jumping contest."

"You have," said Jim. "Well done, Trips."

"Right, I will play Roll Shoving with Jack; best of nine," Chalky said, rolling into position. "Are you ready, Jack?"

Jack nodded.

They rolled towards each other and then shoved with all their might. Chalky rolled backwards in his ball and Jack claimed the first victory.

"First point to me!" he said, raising a bristly paw.

The two went for the second time, first rolling and then shoving. Chalky was moved backwards.

"Yes, I'm two up," Jack said.

At the third attempt, Chalky shoved with all his might, puffing out his cheeks with the effort, and Jack went backwards.

"Yes!" Chalky said.

They rolled and shoved each other again and Jack won the point.

"Yes; three-one to me," Jack said with a grin.

Again, they rolled towards each other and then shoved. Chalky just had the edge and Jack went backwards.

"Yes!" Chalky shouted. "I'm only one in arrears now!"

Could he level the score? They rolled again and he shoved Jack as hard as he could, and Jack went backwards.

"Three-all!" Chalky declared, very pleased with himself.

Rolling and then shoving, Jack managed to win the next point, but Chalky equalised with the one after that.

"Okay," Jack said. "Scores are level; which of us is going to win?"

They rolled towards each other for the last time and shoved until one of them went backwards. It was Chalky.

"I win the Roll Shoving contest," said Jack.

"Yeah," Chalky replied. "Well done, Jack."

"Right, Bobby and I are going to play Circle Diving now," Nutty announced. "Come on Bobby. Are you ready?"

Bobby said he was ready and they both ran around in a circle and then dived to the ground. Nutty hit the ground first.

"Yes! First point to me," Nutty said.

They did the same again, running around in a circle before diving to the ground. This time, it was Bobby who hit the deck first.

"Yes," Bobby said. "Even Stevens!"

"Oh, I must come back stronger," Nutty said as he began to run around in a circle for the next point.

But it was Bobby who hit the ground first.

"Two-one to me," Bobby said.

Nutty knew he would have to try harder and was very determined as he began running in a circle. This time, when they dived, he managed to beat Bobby.

"Yes! Two all," Nutty declared.

He managed to hit the ground first next time as well.

"I'm in the lead now," Nutty said. "Three-two."

Off they went again, running in a circle and diving to the ground. Bobby was first to touch the ground.

"Three all!"

Nutty upped his game, hit the ground first and took the next point.

"Yes. Four-three!" he shouted.

"Let's see which of us will get the next point," said Bobby.

They ran around in a circle, dived to the ground and Nutty just beat Bobby to it.

"I've won the Circle Diving contest," Nutty said, waving his bushy tail with pleasure.

"Yeah," Bobby said. "Well done, Nutty."

"Right, now Stevie and I will play Spin Clapping," Barney announced. "Are you ready, Stevie?"

"Yes, I'm ready," Stevie replied.

Stevie and Barney spun round in a circle and then clapped their paws. Barney made the most noise.

"First point to me," Barney said.

Then they both spun around again and clapped their paws together as hard as they could. This time, Stevie made the most noise.

"Yes," Stevie said, "we're level now."

They spun around once more and clapped their paws together. Barney made the most noise and went a point ahead.

This made Stevie try a bit harder and he won the next point, clapping very loudly.

"Yes," he said. "Level again."

Barney and Stevie spun around and clapped with all their might. Barney clapped loudest and won the next point.

"Three-two to me!" he shouted.

Stevie was a hard badger to beat and he won the next point, making it three all.

Barney was also very competitive and spun around and clapped his paws harder than ever before to take the lead once more.

Again, the contestants spun around and then clapped their paws. Stevie clapped the loudest to make it four all.

"Yes!" Stevie shouted. "This is exciting ... which of us is going to win?"

They spun around in a circle and then clapped their paws like mad, each determined to beat the other, but Barney clapped the loudest.

"Yes. I am the winner of the Spin Clapping contest," Barney declared.

"Yeah, well done, Barney," said Stevie.

"Right; now Pip and I will play Gallop Fast Jumping," said John. "Are you ready, Pip?"

Pip tossed his head. "Ready, John."

Pip and John then galloped along as fast as they could and jumped.

Pip's jump was the longest.

"Yeah!" he said. "I am in the lead."

The two then galloped again and this time John jumped the furthest and levelled the score.

"Yes!"

Pip and John galloped alongside each other and then jumped. John jumped further than Pip and took the lead.

"Yes!" he said. "Two-one to me."

The next time they galloped and jumped, Pip managed to get the longer jump.

"Yeah, level again," he said.

The galloped off again and then jumped. This time, John took the point, giving him the lead back.

"Yes! I lead three-two," he said.

But after the next gallop, Pip jumped the furthest.

"Yeah. Three all," he said.

Pip and John galloped together and both jumped a long way, but John just managed to land ahead of Pip.

"Yes! Four-three."

Next time they jumped, Pip got his nose just in front and again levelled the score.

"Yeah, four all."

Then they set off for the final gallop to see who would jump the furthest and win the final point. It was John.

"I win the Gallop Fast Jumping contest," declared John.

"Yeah," Pip said. "Well done, John."

"Right, now let's applaud the winners of these fights," Baby said and he and the others in the hole applauded himself, Fluffy, Trips, Jack, Nutty, Barney and John.

"Follow me if you want to get out of our hole," Baby said.

Fluffy and his friends said goodbye to the other badgers and followed Baby until they were out of the hole.

"Goodbye, Baby, and thanks" said Fluffy and his friends.

"Okay, bye," Baby said and waved as he left them to go back in the hole with his fellow badgers.

Fluffy and his friends continued their journey to Animal Woods.

"I feel a bit lost," Fluffy said. "I'll ask the cows in that field where we are."

Fluffy's friends followed him through the gate and into the field where the cows were lying down peacefully chewing their cud.

"Hi, my name's Fluffy and these are my friends," said Fluffy. "Do you know where we are by any chance?"

One cow stopped chewing and gazed at Fluffy with large brown eyes. "Yeah," she said, "you're quite close to Animal Woods."

"Really? Oh, well that's where we're going," Fluffy replied.

"Right." The cow nodded at Fluffy and his friends. "Do you want to stay and join our cow disco?"

"Fluffy turned to his friends. "Well?"

They were unanimous. "Yeah!"

Some teenage cows began to dance.

"Teenage moos in a teenage circle, moving around like a cows with a purpose," they said.

"We're mischievous cows," said a teenage cow.

"Yeah," another one agreed.

The other cows then started doing a slow dance. "Walk on, walk on, with hope in our hearts," they sang.

One of the cows then let one rip.

"Walk on … with hope in your fart," they continued, looking at the cow that let off.

Nutty then danced.

"Squirrels are red," said Nutty.

"Good line, Nutty," Fluffy remarked.

Then Pip danced. "Why do only fools and horses dance?" he asked.

"Impressive line," Fluffy said.

"Yeah, it was a good moment," Pip said.

Foley did his dance. "Talk like a cat, move like a cat, twenty-first century cat," he said.

"I love that line," Fluffy told him.

"Yeah, I've got a warm feeling as well," Foley replied.

Then Trips danced. "Memories, happy feline memories," she said.

"Nice line," Fluffy said.

"Yeah. Thanks, Fluffy."

When Barney danced everyone smiled. "Who let the dogs out?" he said.

"Ha ha, that was funny," Fluffy laughed.

"Yeah," Barney said.

Chalky's turn came to dance. "Rat race, rat race … well, hamster race," he said.

"Good one," Fluffy told him.

"Yeah."

Then Fluffy danced. "Rabbit, rabbit, rabbit," he chanted. He looked around at his friends. "That was fun, wasn't it?"

"Yeah, great fun," Foley agreed.

"Are you staying or going to Animal Woods?" one of the cows asked Fluffy.

"We'll stay for now," Fluffy answered.

"So, do you think England will ever win the world cup again?" asked another cow.

"Oh yeah," Fluffy and his friends replied and the other cows nodded in agreement.

"What about Britain's footballers winning gold again?"

Fluffy and his friends and the other cows nodded again. "Yeah!"

"What do you think could fight global warming?" another cow asked.

"A giant flame thrower, to make it rain and end the drought," a cow answered.

"We're mostly water, so more facilities to spread it out," another said.

Fluffy and his friends and the other cows were interested and joined in the discussion.

"More rapeseed fields," said another cow.

"Plant more crops and trees to balance things out," Fluffy suggested.

"We're going for a drink of water. Do you and your friends want some?" one of the cows asked Fluffy.

"No thanks," Fluffy replied.

The cows went and drank from a water trough.

"Are you ready to go now?" Fluffy asked his friends as the cows drank their water.

"Yeah, let's go now," they said.

"Okay. We're off," Fluffy told the nearest cow.

"Bye," the cows said, swishing their tails.

"Bye," Fluffy and his friends replied, as they moved off to continue their journey to Animal Woods.

They hadn't walked far, when they met a peacock strutting along proudly.

"Hi," Fluffy said. Show us your tail feathers?"

"Okay, my pleasure," the peacock replied and fanned out his colourful tail feathers.

"Magnificent," Fluffy said.

"Yeah," his friends agreed, "beautiful colours."

"Where are you lot off to?" the peacock asked.

"Animal Woods," Fluffy replied.

"Okay, well you're very close."

"Yeah, we thought we must be," Fluffy said. "So, do you get any other animals passing by?"

"Yes, there are birds flying over all the time and hedgehogs pass by as well."

"Really? How often is that?" Fluffy asked.

"Every week."

"Okay," Fluffy said.

"What sort of things are you into?" Foley wanted to know.

"Other than speaking to passers-by, I like dancing," the peacock replied.

"Do you have any kids?" Pip asked him.

"No. Why do you ask?"

Pip shrugged. "Just wondered."

"Do you listen to music?" Nutty asked.

"Yeah, I eavesdrop on music from passing cats," the peacock said with a sideways glance at Foley and Trips.

"Right."

"Well, we're off now," Fluffy said. "Bye."

"Bye, nice to have met you," the peacock replied.

"That was a nice chat we had," Fluffy remarked to his friends.

"Yeah," his friends agreed as they continued walking to Animal Woods.

"Are you all excited about being so close to Animal Woods?" Fluffy asked his friends.

"Yeah," they answered. "Are you?"

"Yeah, I'm excited as well," Fluffy replied.

Fluffy and his friends were walking at the side of a road. After a short distance, they tried to cross the road but there were a lot of cars going past.

"We'll have to wait until these cars have passed," Fluffy told his friends.

"Yeah," his friends agreed and waited patiently for the cars to go past. When the road was clear, they crossed over and continued walking to Animal Woods.

In a matter of minutes, they arrived at their destination.

"Here we are," Fluffy said, looking at the sign that said ANIMAL WOODS.

"Yeah," his friends replied, pleased to be there.

The words on the sign had been put there by the animals.

"Let's explore this place," Fluffy said.

"Yeah," his friends agreed and they all went off to begin exploring.

"Look," Fluffy said, "There are some woodland creatures." He and his friends walked towards them.

"Hi," said Fluffy to the woodland creatures.

"Hi," the woodland creatures replied. "Did you see Animal Woods on a sign that we made?"

"Yeah, we did," Fluffy said and his friends nodded in agreement.

"We'll leave you to have a look round, then," said one of the woodland creatures.

"Thanks," said Fluffy. "Bye."

"Bye!"

Fluffy and his friends took a look around. "There are some trees," Fluffy said. "Shall we take a whizz?"

"Ooh, yeah," his friends agreed and went behind the trees.

"That was good," Foley said as they re-emerged from behind the trees.

"Yeah!"

"Shall we have a run now?" Fluffy asked his friends.

"Yeah," his friends agreed, lining up with Fluffy for a run.

Fluffy was the winner. "Yes! I won," he said.

"Well done, Fluffy," said his friends.

"Let's go and find something to eat now," Fluffy said.

"Yeah," his friends agreed as they went in search of some food.

They were lucky and found some food, and soon afterwards, found the perfect place to stop for a while to cook and eat their meal. Fluffy and his friends found some stones and enough dry wood to make a barbecue.

Fluffy lit the fire and they cooked all of the delicious morsels they had found in the wood. When they had finished their meal, Fluffy and his friends sat around the fire's embers, talking about their journey to Animal Woods.

They talked late into the night; it had been a long journey for Fluffy Rabbit and his friends and they had many adventures to talk about.